To my mother Cathy, my father Erin, and my Aunt Florrie; thanks for every sacrifice you've ever made for me. To my wife and kids, thanks for continuing to motivate and inspire me to be great. To my siblings, I hope I've made you proud.

—Nicholas Sampson

www.mascotbooks.com

There's a Person on Top of My Bed

For more information, please contact:

Mascot Books
560 Herndon Parkway #120
Herndon, VA 20170
info@mascotbooks.com

Second Printing. This Mascot Books edition printed in 2019.

Library of Congress Control Number: 2017906331

CPSIA Code: PRT0919B
ISBN-13: 978-1-68401-255-8

Printed in the United States

THERE'S A PERSON ON TOP OF MY BED

Written by Nicholas Sampson

Illustrated by Nidhom

I first saw her two days ago
    while I was just about to go to sleep.

She was swinging those things in front of me.
    I think the people call them feet.

It was my first time seeing one,
    so I thought it was kind of neat.

The way those things called toes
    were wiggling to an imaginary beat.

I wanted to get a better look,
    so I scooted closer in order to see.

Because I've never seen toes on the foot of a person,
    but I've heard rumors that sounded strange to me.

I heard if you tickled the bottom of a person's foot,
they would do this crazy thing called laugh.

My friend Roger said it was true,
and that he had proof with a photograph.

I heard that a person's foot gets dirty
and smelly from my best friend Sam.

He said it was because of this stuff that sounded delicious.
I think he called it Toe Jam.

Now the curiosity is bothering me,
  and I'm too close to turn back.

I took a deep inhale, and I must admit,
  what Sam said was indeed a fact.

The smell was something I can't forget.
  To describe it might give you a clue.

It smelled like a combination of rotten eggs
  and a pig's pen at the zoo.

Now there's one more thing that
    I needed to know whether or not was true.

If I tickled the bottom of a person's foot,
    what would it say or do?

The suspense and continuing thought
    of this gave me butterflies inside.

I made up my mind: on the count of three,
    there's no more thinking, it's tickle time!

One! Two! Three!

I heard this faint sound
    that got louder by the touch.

It started out with a ha-ha-ha,
    but ended far louder than such.

All of a sudden she fell on the floor, her laughter too great to contain.
The next thing that happened was unexpected, and I must admit, a little insane.

While she was rolling on the floor with laughter, she turned and we locked eyes.
We stared at each other for a second or two, both a little amused and surprised.

I gave her a small smile,
    hoping that I would receive one back.

But instead, a look of fear showed on her face,
    as if she thought I would attack.

I wanted to show her I was friendly, so I said, "Hello, my name's Ted."
But instead of introducing herself, she yelled,

"Mom, there's a MONSTER under my bed!"

At this point I said, "Calm down!
    There's no reason to scream and yelp.

Why don't you tell me why you're so scared of me?
    Maybe there's some way that I can help!"

She told me she heard all monsters were bad
and that they fill little kids with fright.

She said she heard we had sharp teeth
and that we eat little kids at night.

She said she heard monsters hide in closets
and like to make scary sounds.

She also said she heard we steal little children
and take them back to Monster Town.

"**Now** **wait a minute!**" I said to her.
"That stuff you said, can you please show me proof?

Just because someone says something about you,
doesn't actually mean it's the truth.

You said you heard all monsters are bad
and we like to scare little kids.

But what if you heard that simply because someone
doesn't understand what being different is?"

"You said you heard we have sharp teeth and that we eat little kids at night.
But truth be told, my teeth are nice and all I like to eat are burger bites.

You said that monsters like to hide in closets and make noises that scare.
But the only reason we hide in closets is because it's so much warmer in there."

"The saying goes, don't judge a book by its cover, and from my experience as a monster, this holds true.

So can we start our introduction over? If you promise not to judge me, I promise I won't judge you."

Deal?

Deal!

If you form your own opinions of people instead of judging them based off the opinions of others, you'd be amazed at how many friendships you can build.

About the Author

Nicholas was raised in Rocky Ford, Georgia, where he learned at an early age the power of imagination. Growing up in the country allowed Nicholas to understand that you could do or be anything you wanted to be in life if you could imagine it and devise a plan to achieve it. Nicholas has always enjoyed writing and drawing as a way to express himself. Nicholas is a military veteran, a husband, and a father of two beautiful girls.

CONTACT HANDLE

Twitter: @IamNickSampson

Gmail: IamNickSampson@gmail.com